What Would Whitney Do?

By: Annie Hensley

For Whitney and Karia who are always down for wine and cake.

CHAPTER ONE: TWO PUMP CHUMP

"All I'm saying," I tell her as I stuff a tortilla chip in my mouth and attempt to talk around it. "Is that you took 'Fuck the Police' seriously. And while I am happy for you, it kinda makes me throw up in my mouth."

My best friend in the entire world, Jo, smiles back at me and sets her mojito down. She makes a big show of licking her lips before replying, "You're damn right I did."

Gosh, I just love her, and I am happy for her and Gauge, truly. Her path to happiness was not easy but she made it. She not only had to deal with being cheated on by Brad that Bastard; but he cheated with her sister. Last month they announced their engagement. Oh, and then she had to bail me out of jail with the help of a somewhat bitchy bondsman. But now 6 months later, we can at least laugh about it.

"I know, I know." I hold my hands up before she can launch into another story about their wonderful sex life.

"Whitney, you'll find someone." She gives me a little smirk. "Especially now that you're through with your community service."

I give her the finger but it's not out of malice. Thanks to a lenient judge and Becky talking Brad into dropping the charges, I was able to get off with a small fine and community service. Not that Brad had much of a choice considering Becky deleted the evidence against me. It surprised the hell out of me when Jo told me about it. I mean, we had gotten into a rumble that would have made fight club happy, not too long before that.

However, I still got in trouble because the apartment manager had a stick up his ass. He felt that the people needed to know that trespassing and vandalism was not something the apartment complex would not tolerate. Someone should remove the stick and beat him like a pinata.

"Truth. But the kinda guys I have seen the past couple months are not giving me much hope at all!"

Jo smiles and flags the waitress over. "Before we get into this, I am going to need another drink."

"Are you serious?" Jo is laughing so hard and loudly that people at neighboring tables are glaring at us. It is a common thing wherever we go.

"Shhhh!" I shush her. "Yes, I'm serious."

Once she calms down, she begins ticking a list off of her fingers. "Ok so just to break it down; you have been out with a want to be rapper, a guy who thinks he is a cowboy, a polygamist and that does not even cover the "two-pump chump."

When she puts it like that, I just want to slide under the table. I am such a loser. Now I just need Peter Dinklage to come up to me and call me Second Place. I mean yeah that is essentially true. I feel the need to explain a bit more to make myself feel better. She did forget to count the Mama's boy though and I wasn't about to remind her.

"I mean Pryce did have a job other than putting up videos of himself on Instagram. But yeah, he wanted to be a rapper."

I take a drink of my margarita. "He wasn't terrible or anything, but a rap career is not in that man's future. I asked him to lose my number after he sent me a video of him rapping about our date. "

Jo snorts, "Did it go something like: "Hey Whitney thanks for the date, for our next one I can't wait?"

She was pretty damn close, and it was annoying. "Something like that." I shrug. "Anyway, Ben, he probably would have made a good cowboy."

"Hold that thought." Jo answered her ringing phone and I tried not to resent her for having someone in her life other than me. It was somewhat pathetic to admit, but she was not only my best friend but my only friend. I am also an only child, with parents who live halfway across the country. I'm alone except for the woman sitting across from me.

"I love you too boo." She hung up and smiled at me sheepishly. "Gauge." As though I hadn't already figured that out for myself. "Ok tell me about Ben."

I quickly launch into a diatribe about Ben. "I mean sure he looked great in those wranglers, but he doesn't own horses. Plus, he chews and it's so gross."

Jo nods, "I don't get why guys don't understand the level of disgustingness that comes from chewing." She signals to the waitress, which signals to me that the evening is coming to an end.

"I have to get going," she explains as she pulls out her credit card and slides it into the little black folder. "Ever since Natalie took maternity leave, things have been completely crazy at work."

"Have you seen the baby?" I slide my own card over for my bill as the waitress scoops them up and walks away.

"That baby, dude, seriously I want to throw away my birth control and rape the shit out of Gauge." She laughs and I have to laugh at the picture she just painted. "But with my luck the baby would be ugly, so I'll continue to be safe."

I shake my head at her and thank the waitress who has returned. As she walks away and we both sign our slips, I look at her mischievously. "Am I going to take the blame for that when it happens too?"

She starts laughing and not any laugh either, she is doing her retarded banshee laugh and I instantly regret being so damn funny. It is true though, when she made her move on Gauge, she claims to have asked herself "what would Whitney do?" Once she finally contains herself, we both leave the booth.

"You can't still be bothered by that?" It's more of a question than a statement as we reach the parking lot.

"I'm not. I just enjoy giving you shit." I hug her goodbye and walk to my car.

"You'll find someone Whitney, and not a two-pump chump either!"

She laughs before climbing into her car and I can only shake my head as the elderly couple getting out of their own car stares at me; no doubt appalled by what they heard.

As I head back to my apartment, I turn my radio down and think back on the guys I have dated. Although there are plenty that I felt had no value, I had had high hopes for the two-pump chump. I mean obviously, I went to bed with him. I'm not a ho that swings from dick to dick.

But alas, he was a huge let down. I may have believed him when he told me it was because he was so turned on by me. Or when he said it was only because it was our first time but the third time it happened; I had had enough. Goodbye Seth. I pull into my designated space and walk to my second-floor apartment.

It's a small two bedroom but its home and I feel a sense of relief as I open the door. I tried to have a roommate once but honestly, I hate people. I shut the door, drop my purse on the floor and collapse on the futon. Plus, I like my privacy. I stand back up and strip to my bra and panties, then lay back down on the futon, wincing when my bare skin touches the cold black metal.

I do need to find someone, but the thing is I don't really know how. It's not like I have a ton of free time. Plus, I really don't want to do the whole internet dating thing again. That's how I ended up with the list Jo was laughing about.

"Fuck it." I pull myself up into a sitting position, completely ungraceful and not without struggle. I reach for my phone, remember it's in my purse and get up to get it. Sitting back on the futon, I edit my information on all the dating apps I told Jo I had deleted.

"No Two Pump Chumps," is now listed at the bottom of my bio. There! Now Prince Charming will fall into my lap. I set the phone on the coffee table and go to shower.

<u>**CHAPTER TWO: ORAL IS MORAL**</u>

"I don't know why I'm doing this!" I practically shriek into the phone as I step into my black wedges.

"You'll be fine." Jo is trying to reassure me, but I can also tell that she wants me to stop whining so she can go back to making out with Gauge.

"Yeah, yeah." I take a last look in the mirror, spin in a circle so my black and gray sundress billowed gently.

"How do you look?" Jo asks and I can hear Gauge making a smart-ass comment in the background, though I can't quite make it out.

"Eh, I'd do me." I grab my purse and head to the door.

"If the date sucks, you may have to." She cracks up at her own joke and I hang up on her. I have things to do. I walk out of the apartment to meet my blind date.

****

"That's really fascinating," I say for the fifth time in twenty minutes. I smile as I say it, but it's as forced as this date. Who knew that Hank would be so damn boring?

"Thank you, Whitney. I think that it's important work that we are doing." He beams, a piece of his dinner stuck in his perfect white teeth. His smile was the main thing that had me agreeing to this date but now I don't even want to look at him.

"Um, you have something right here." I tap on my own teeth for emphasis and then watch stupefied as he pulls a sandwich baggie full of flossers out of his jacket pocket. He immediately goes to work right there at the table while I struggle with my gag reflex.

"You should always be prepared." He states as he wiggles the stick between teeth. "So, I have spent a lot of time talking about myself, please tell me about you."

Desperate to put my thoughts on anything other than him flossing at the dinner table, I take a sip of my water. "I own a little shop over on Roberts Avenue."

"Really? That's neat." He makes a sucking sound and yes, he actually fucking swallowed his spit and whatever he just dislodged from his gums. Before he can say anything else, I excuse myself to the bathroom.

I enter the first stall and sit carefully on the toilet, folding my dress like a lady so it doesn't dip into the toilet. "What the fuck?" I mumble to myself. I mean he seemed normal on his profile. A good-looking guy with dark hair and bright blue eyes that were to my surprise not the result of contacts. He was clean shaven with flawless skin and dimples. He runs a non-profit, doesn't smoke or drink and wears deodorant. I should have known it was too good to be true. And what kinda name is Hank anyway?

I force myself to leave the stall, I face myself in the mirror as I wash my hands. I study my reflection, noting that it too has changed in the past six months. I have let my hair grow long and no longer put the red in it. "You will get through this date." I order myself and then dry my hands. Before I can change my mind, I march back to the table.

"Hey." The floss sticks have disappeared, and he beams at me as I slide into my chair. "I waited for you."

I look at him in confusion. "Waited for me?"

"Yeah." He gestures at the plate in front of him. "I have not taken a bite since you left."

He looks so proud that I actually feel sorry for him. "Oh, great. Thank you." I pick up my fork and twirl my pasta. Normally I love eating at any restaurant with good alfredo but for some insane reason; I just can't tonight.

"Tell me about your shop." He takes a bite of his lasagna. "What kind of things do you sell?" His mouth is full of noodles and cheese and I'm once again fighting the urge to gag.

"It's actually a thrift shop. It's called Thrifty with Whitney." I take another drink of my water but push my plate away. I'm done with my dinner and with Hank.

"Clever name." He takes a bite out of a breadstick. "Do you make pretty good money?"

"Enough to get me by." What a dick. You don't ask someone that. A few more minutes, I tell myself. Just a few more minutes.

"Are you finished?" He gestures to my mostly full plate.

I nod. "Yes, I guess my eyes were bigger than my stomach."

He gestures to the waitress and asks for the check. "Oh, and can we get a box please?"

I hadn't planned on taking the leftovers home, but I guess I am now. The waitress returns with the little black folder and a square white Styrofoam box. I'm never sure how the payment thing works on blind dates, so I reach in my purse for my wallet.

"Oh no, I got it." Hank pulls out his card and slides it in the slot before handing it back to the waitress. "The lady doesn't pay, you silly goose."

Silly goose? I literally have no words, so I smile my thanks and start shoveling my pasta into the to go box. Once I am done, I close the lid and scoot it over to the side of the table.

The waitress scoops up the book on her way by, her blond ponytail swaying side to side as she walks towards the back. I pull some cash out of my wallet and leave the tip.

"So," Hank leans forward and lowers his voice. "Do you want to go back to my place?"

He's fucking kidding me, right? I feel the little bit of food I managed to eat rolling around in my stomach. "I'm sorry, but I'm going to have to pass."

He leans further over, almost pressing his chest into his discarded plate. "Oh, come on. I'm not expecting anything. I just don't want the night to end quite yet."

I stand up relieved when the waitress comes back with his card. She looks as bored as I am sure I did earlier. She smiles a halfhearted smile as I grab my to go box and purse.

Hank frowns at me as he also stands. He's almost a full head taller than me, even with the wedges, which was another reason I was interested. We make our way out of the restaurant and I hesitate before walking to my car. Figuring that he wasn't going to be easily shook off, I head to my Veloster. Once I reach it, I turn to face him.

"It was nice meeting you Hank." I put my hand out for him to shake but he instead takes it and brings it to his lips. I shudder and want desperately to yank my hand back.

"It was so nice to meet you as well." He lets go of my hand and steps forward essentially trapping me. "I like that you don't want to go home with me. I like a girl with morals."

"Um, yeah. I have morals." It has nothing to do with the fact that you are a creepy gross pig, I think to myself. "Do you mind stepping back? I need to get going. Thank you so much for dinner." Plus, if you don't back up, I'm gonna smash my leftovers in your face.

He steps back with a sigh of regret. "You know, you can follow me to my place, and we can get to know each other better."

"I have a lot of work to do." Translation – I am not going to your house and having sex with you. Now or ever.

"Oral is moral." He says it with a smile.

My eyes go wide and my jaw drops. I gape at him stupidly before asking in disbelief, "excuse me?"

"If you are worried about having sex before marriage or if you think it's in poor taste to put out on the first date; we can do oral." He shrugs. "You can just blow me. I'm completely fine with it."

The gall of this man. Deciding to take the high road I reach in my purse and press the button on my key fob. I open the driver door then turn and look at him.

"You know Hank. As tempting as it sounds to finish a less than wonderful evening, by putting your probably less than impressive penis in my mouth; I'd rather go home and watch the ending of Marley and Me. Or maybe My Sister's Keeper in a continuous loop."

I toss my purse into the passenger seat and with a little more care, set down the to go box. When I go to slide in the seat, I notice Hank still standing there, his face with ridged with anger.

"A word of advice little girl." Though he is still smiling, there is malice in his eyes. "If you don't want people to treat you like an easy lay, don't go advertising that you want it." He does a quick look around the parking lot then lowers his voice. "No two pump chumps, right? As if that doesn't scream whore."

I have no words as he walks away.

CHAPTER THREE: SATAN'S BUTTHOLE

"I think if we put it over to the corner, below the corner shelf," I point to a wooden teal shelf. "We can create a little reading nook and perhaps sell the whole set together."

Beth nods and together we move the fluffy gray wedge chair. It's not as easy as it sounds. Beth or Bethany depending on who is speaking to her is a slight girl. She looks almost delicate and any physical labor is a struggle. But her organizational skills are amazing.

I'm in a bad mood but trying not to show it. I'm still angry about my date the night before. Mainly because he was right. Fucking Hank. I mean I may as well have written that I would be conducting auditions for stamina. Beth, bless her is amazingly astute and has kept her bubbly personality to herself for the most part. Nothing annoys me more than when I am an angry mess and people are all smiles and giggles.

She tucks her blond streaked hair behind one ear and her blue eyes light up. "That looks really good!"

I nod. "Yes, it does." I walk over to the door, flip the lock and the open sign. "You want to put the rug out front? And maybe one of those little end tables with that new lamp we got in?"

She goes to do as I asked, and I make my way to the back room and the coffee maker. I deleted all of my dating apps and that was that. I hadn't even called Jo to give her an update or returned any of her messages. In a way, I'm ashamed. In others I am forced to admit that I somewhat had it coming. I shake my head. That is personal and doesn't belong here at work.

I pour two cups of coffee. One with so much creamer the coffee is almost cold and the other straight black with one teaspoon of sugar. Perhaps that is why Beth is so thin. I am not exactly fat, but you can definitely tell that I enjoy good food. I take the cups with me and join her behind the counter. She is counting out the drawer but smiles her thanks at me when I set the cup down next to her. Normally Saturdays are our busiest days, so we are both bracing ourselves for the rush. But for now, all is calm.

"Done." Beth slides the drawer back into the register, initials the count slip and hands it to me.

"Thanks." I tuck it into the file folder to my right. I wouldn't necessarily consider Beth a friend, but I do try to keep things friendly. It's a system that has worked well for us the last few years. "How was your day off?"

She grinned sheepishly and picked up her coffee cup. "It was good. I did some laundry, wrote a paper and um, went to dinner with Brandon."

Brandon is this guy that she has seen off and on. She tends to end things and then go right back to see him. Something about him liking other girls Instagram posts. I don't really keep up with it because, we aren't really friends and it's none of my business.

"Oh. "I take a drink of my coffee, debating if I should tell her about my own dinner. Yeah, I'm not going to. "That sounds nice."

"How was your date?"

I whip my head a little too fast in her direction. "What date?"

She kinda laughs as she meets my eyes. "I saw you last night at Vinny's. Looked like a date to me."

I flush until I am as red as the blinking sale sign in the window. "It wasn't the greatest."

She gives me a knowing look but before she can impart any words of wisdom or consolation, the front door dings.

"Saved by the bell," I mutter as she goes to assist the two old ladies coming through the door.

The Hansen twins set the tone for the rest of the day. We have a nonstop flow of customers and by the time three o clock rolls around we are both beat. Beth hauls the end table in from outside and locks the door behind her.

"Wow, what a day!" She brushes her hair out of her face. "Ready to do clean up?"

Saturdays are deep cleaning days. Every Saturday after closing, we change into our crappiest clothes, pull our hair up and clean every inch of the shop. It's also why we close at three. But, spending another couple hours with Beth and her nosy ass questions, doesn't seem like a good idea.

"How about you balance the drawer and take the deposit? I think I can handle it today." I try to come off as casual and as a boss trying to be nice.

"Are you sure?" But her eyes have already lit up and I can tell she's eager to leave.

"Yeah, I'm good." Or I will be when I take my frustration out on innocent dust bunnies. "Go on and get out of here. You worked hard today."

"Thanks Whitney." She's already pulled the drawer out of the register. "I'll lock up on the way out."

I smile my thanks and head into the small bathroom in the back of the store. This is the one that she and I use. The nicer, handicap accessible one up front is for the customers. I grab my duffle bag and remove a t-shirt and cutoffs I'm about to change into. I remove my capris and loose tank and fold them nicely into the bag. I slip off my sandals, curse at myself for being stupid and pull the clothes back out. I set the sandals down, then the clothes and step into the shorts. The Animal House t shirt goes over my head and before it's fully settled, I'm grabbing my converse and socks tucked under the shelf.

After they are on, I face myself in the mirror. I splash cold water on my face, removing most of my make up when I pat it dry. I throw my hair in a messy bun best reserved for those that live in Whoville and walk out the door. My purse in hanging on a hook next to the supply closet and I reach in it now for my headphones. Beth pops in, says goodbye and heads out.

With Lizzo blasting in my ears, I tackle the customer bathroom first. I sweep, scrub the toilet, wash the mirrors and the sink. I am scrubbing the shit out of the porcelain tile on my hands and knees when someone taps me on the shoulder. I yelp, spin around and jump to my feet in what seems like one solid movement. My heart is thundering in my chest and I hope I calm down before it explodes. I experience a prickle of fear however when I notice that the one who tapped me is a man; a stranger that I have never met, and I am completely alone in an empty store.

I yank my headphones out of my ears and let them dangle around my neck. "Can I help you?" My voice is steady even though everything else about me is not.

"I'm sorry if I scared you." He looks me up and down and smiles. "I didn't realize you had headphones in."

I'm feeling slightly claustrophobic and want desperately to get out of the bathroom. Preferably into the front of the store with all the windows. I remove the yellow rubber gloves I am wearing and drop them on the floor.

"We are closed for the day. Do you mind me asking how you got in?" I step towards him and am relieved when he steps back to allow me to pass. Now that he is no longer in shadow, I feel better that there's a face to match the voice.

And what a face. He is absolutely gorgeous. My mouth goes completely dry and I feel my face flame. I'm well aware of how I look. I am a sweaty, dirty mess. I'm in shitty clothes with wild hair and scarce make up if any. In short, I look like Satan's butthole. And him. Inwardly I sigh. He looks like fricking Thor. Like he could be his twin. I shake my head and walk quickly to the front.

He smiles when I turn and face him at the counter, and I swear I felt something click.

"I'm sorry but the sign still say open and the door was unlocked." He shrugged, his t shirt showing off the well-formed shoulders and making me inwardly drool. "I was interested in the whitewashed vanity."

Two realizations hit me, and I'm equally upset about both of them. First, Beth didn't lock the damn door which pisses me off and second, he must have a wife or girlfriend if he wants a vanity. That's incredibly disappointing. However, I shake it off. I am a business owner, albeit a filthy one and I need to act like one.

"Yes, we close at three on Saturdays, but I can certainly show it to you if you'd like." I began walking towards it.

"Oh, no. I've seen it." I stop and look at him quizzically. "I was looking at it while I was up here all alone. I want to buy it, but I can wait until you open on Monday."

I smile, knowing full well the vanity will make a great sale and free up space for the antique cook stove I want to bring in. "You're here now, so let's just go ahead."

I walk over to the vanity where I remove the tag and take special care to avoid the oval mirror. I go back behind the counter and key in the price. He hands me his card and I swipe it, flushing again when I realize it was a chip. I insert it in the machine and then realize he had asked me something.

"I'm sorry what?"

"I asked if your boss was going to be upset that I am in here after hours." His blue eyes seem actually concerned and for some reason it touches me. "Or are you going to get in trouble for not locking the door?"

I remove his card and the sales slips. "Actually, the owner does like things to be ran a certain way; but she's not overally harsh."

He signs the slip. "Good." He puts the card back in his plain black wallet and slides it in the pocket of his jeans. "Do you mind if I pick it up Monday afternoon? I'm not in my truck today."

I grab a piece of paper, write SOLD on it with a sharpie and go set it on the vanity. "Not a problem. Is your wife going to be fine with waiting for it though?"

He laughs. Yes, even his laugh is sexy. Why are all the good men taken? "Actually, it's for my mother. She drives my father crazy with her make-up and perfumes all over the place so he's making her a little dressing room. Gauge told me you had a vanity down here and since it's her birthday next week." He shrugged again. "Here I am."

I gape at him. "You know Gauge?" How could he have a friend this fricking hot and not tell me? Jo was definitely getting a phone call after he left. Well after I finished cleaning.

"Yeah, we went to high school together." As though a light came on, he looks at me quizzically. "Wait a minute. Are you Whitney?"

"I am." I put a handout, then pull it back remembering I haven't washed my hands.

"I'm Chris." He doesn't acknowledge the fake handshake and I'm grateful. "So, you own this place?"

"I do." I keep the fact that I scraped and saved and busted my ass for seven years to get it where it is to myself

"It's a nice place. The quality of your products is top notch." He runs a hand across the vanity top, a light gray marble and my skin breaks out in goose bumps as I watch his long lean fingers. "I guess I will see you on Monday. Thank you, Whitney. Have a nice night."

I follow him to the door where I lock the dead bolt behind him and turn the sign to closed. I lean against the door, my mind a jumble of thoughts. He looked like Chris Hemsworth. His name was Chris. He didn't have a wife, but did he have someone? He cared about his mother. He smelled nice. He was tall but not freakishly so. He didn't try to haggle. He has a car and a truck. He was a nice dresser. Gauge has a hot friend. Jo didn't tell me. He saw you like this and didn't bolt.

I look down and study myself. Eh, I've looked worse. But damn, why did he have to see me at the worst possible time. I *really* do look like Satan's butthole. It's a fairly accurate assessment. I shove from the door and head back into the bathroom where I stand in the doorway. I smile when I realize that me being on my hands and knees in the cut offs may have made up a little for the way the front of me looked.

I sigh on pull on the gloves again. I need to finish up here so I can call Jo and ask her what the story was with that fine piece of male.

CHAPTER FOUR: THE 'I' IS SILENT

"Hey Whitney, what are you doing here?"

I guess showing up at Jo's house still dirty straight from work was a bit extreme, but I felt we could cover more ground in person. But normally I just walk in like I own the joint. The only reason I knocked this time is because of the unknown Toyota pickup parked out front. Something about the way she asked that kinda stings.

"I wanted to talk to you, but if this is a bad time, I guess just call me later." I turn and start to walk away feeling dejected, my excitement about gathering information about Chris completely gone.

"Shit. Hold up." Jo follows me down the driveway. "I'm sorry. Gauge is here and we invited his cousin over for dinner. You just caught me off guard." She wrinkles her nose. "And you kinda stink."

I flip her off and keep walking. "It's Saturday, dick. You know I clean on Saturdays."

"I know Whit." She puts a hand on my shoulder and when I stop, she steps in front of me. "What's going on?"

"Babe?"

We both turn to the porch where Gauge is standing in the doorway. "Oh, hey Whitney. You guys head in it's time to eat."

Jo and I look at each other and she shrugs. "Guess you're invited to dinner. Come on."

Unsure I look down at my dirty clothes and then back at her. "It's totally fine Whitney, Gauge's cousin is actually pretty cool."

I follow her up the driveway. I can't pump them for information in front of a complete stranger. I suppose I could, but I am trying to turn my psycho down. At least in front of strangers.

A beautiful brunette with hair down to her waist is standing next to the couch. I not only study her but also the new couch. Jo finally got rid of the one that Brad, that bastard had bent Becky over, and I am so glad. Remembering my manners, I introduce myself.

"Hey, I'm Whitney."

"Hi, Whitney." She turns towards me and I can see a name tag pinned to her chest. K-A-R-I-A. No clue how to pronounce it so I wait. "I'm Karia."

"Oh, ok, that's a lot easier to say than I was expecting."

She laughs and pulls me into a hug. It's awkward yet strangely nice. She steps back, her brown eyes glowing with mischief. "My parents are weird. The 'I' is silent. They should have spelled it K A R A but oh well."

She pulls her name tag off and slides it in the back of her jeans. "I work at the preschool and always forget to take this stupid thing off."

I smile. "I didn't realize there were so many different ways to spell names."

We both head towards the kitchen when Jo hollers at us. I didn't even realize she had left us alone until now. "I didn't know there was preschool on the weekends."

She sits down at the table. "We offer preschool on Saturdays to help out the parents. Not everyone works 9-5 Monday through Friday. We don't do like six days or anything like that. The kids that come on Saturday don't come on Mondays."

Gauge and Jo are piling burgers and brauts and every possible condiment on the table. My offer to help is ignored and they continue to pile buns and potato salad and even baked beans. Karia is still talking about the preschool and though I'm not trying to be rude; I am tuning her out. I'm trying to find a way to get information about Chris without seeming obvious.

When they finally sit down and we being making our plates, I aim for casual. "So, I think I met a friend of yours today Gauge." Perfect.

"Oh, yeah? Who's that?" He's watching as Jo makes her plate. He's trying to keep the amusement off his face and she carefully makes sure nothing is touching. It's a Jo thing and one that will never change.

"Chris." I squirt ketchup and mustard on a jalapeño cheddar braut. "Came in to buy a vanity you told him about."

"So, he did go get it?" He bites into his burger and chases it down with a sip of Twisted Tea. "He asked me the other day when we were playing basketball if I knew of any place that had a nice one. So naturally, being the amazing good friend that I am I sent him your way." He winks at Jo then turns back to me. "I get commission, right?"

"What's commission?"

Karia laughs at my question. "Tell me about your store Whitney."

So, I do. Despite her being essentially a stranger who is keeping me from interrogating Jo and Gauge, I like her. She's easy without trying too hard and actually seems to listen when someone talks. Unlike me earlier in the evening.

"I'll have to come check it out! Do you do consignments?" She's got a beaming smile that makes her look super young.

"We do." I turn my attention back to the happy couple. Though I can acknowledge my bad behavior and feel guilty about it, doesn't mean I'm going to change it. "So, what's his story?"

Jo snorts and sets down the White Claw she was about to drink. "You mean is he single?"

"Absofuckinglutely. Have you seen that man?"

Gauge laughs. "He's pretty good looking. I've thought about going gay for that man."

This time it's Karia who snorts and then all of us are laughing.

"He's single. His last break up was rough to say the least though so I don't know that you should chase him." Gauge is still smiling though his eyes are somber.

"I wasn't going to chase him. I don't run after men." Though sometimes I consider a light jog or a power walk. "I just wanted to know."

Jo studies me for a minute then asked, "did you look like that when you met him?"

"Unfortunately, I did."

"Well then, what are you worried about Gauge? There's not a chance in hell he'd be interested." She smiles sweetly.

"Bitch." I throw a pickle at her.

****

"Ugh!" I shimmy out of my jeans that were just a touch too tight and leave them crumpled up on the floor.

I throw myself on the bed in frustration. I want to look good when Chris comes to pick up his order and none of my clothes are doing me any favors. Perhaps I am being a bit ridiculous, and maybe a little bit dramatic but still. I did spend most of Sunday pampering myself. Face mask, hair mask, shaved everything below my eyebrows; I mean I need to be ready for anything.

I force myself up, stand in the closet, close my eyes and pull out the first thing my hand touches. Looks like I am wearing a dress today. I pull the polo I had on off and pull the dress over my head. It brings out the green in my eyes and makes me legs look tan. I slip on little black sandals and go into the bathroom where I start on my makeup. The need to look flawless is overwhelming. I have to prove that I don't always look like swamp ass.

I have been referred to once or twice as a high maintenance type of girl. But those types of bitches don't understand that I can be ready, fully made up in less than half an hour. High maintenance my ass. Once my primer and foundation is on, I do my eyebrows. I once heard that the eyes are the windows of the face, so obviously the eyebrows are the curtains. Super important. From eyebrows I do contour, eye shadow and mascara. I spritz myself with setting spray and head out the door.

My phone chimes at me as I slide behind the wheel. It appears that Karia, the I is silent has sent me a friend request on Facebook. I accept it, put on my sunglasses and head to work. Today is going to be a good day. I can feel it.

<u>**CHAPTER FIVE: THE ZING**</u>

Today can suck twenty-eight dicks. It's 4:30 and anything that could go wrong at the shop has. We had a mother who is incapable of watching her children, come in and instead of making a sale, I'm making repairs. We apparently have a mouse running around so there's that. The sink in the bathroom is leaking and on top of all that, Chris has still not come in.

I have taken great pains to stay fresh looking all day and does he even have the decency to bring his fine ass in here and look at me? I rub at my temples and pray that the minor throbbing doesn't develop into a full-fledged migraine. I have let Beth alone up front and am sitting in the office, supposedly working on inventory.

The truth is I am getting more and more angry and don't trust myself to not explode at the next person that annoys me in any way. I'm chugging a Monster and snacking on chips when I hear a knock at the door. Beth opens the door and pops her head in cautiously.

"There's someone up front asking for you. Do you want me to say that you are out?" She smiles sympathetically.

"No, I'll be right there." I wait until she shuts the door before I let the smile light up my face. This is it! He is here. I jump up and desperately brush at the chip crumbs chilling on my chest. I reach in my purse for a piece of gum. Just before walking out the door, I fluff my hair and spray my perfume. He isn't going to know what hit him.

I walk, no, I saunter down the hall like a woman on a mission and enter the shop floor like a runway model. I'm fully prepared to see that well-muscled god waiting for me at the counter but instead to my crushing disappointment I see Karia. The disappointment is like a sharp punch to the stomach. I force myself to look pleased and walk up to her.

"Hey girl," she beams at me. "Your store is beautiful."

My shame hits and I force myself to be nice. Yeah, she's not a hot man or even a customer but she's here and she's great.

"Thank you! Would you like a tour?"

"Sure, but first, I want this vase."

Beth takes it from her and rings her up. "I'll leave it up here in the bag for you whenever you are ready."

"Thanks." Karia is all smiles as I show her around the shop, I bust my ass for every day. "This place is awesome, Whitney. Normally thrift shops are dark and dirty looking, but yours is full of light and gorgeous things."

We are in the little kitchen, sipping on cold cherry cokes I pulled out of the fridge. Beth walks around the corner. "Hey boss, it's five and I'm gonna take off. Want me to lock up?"

That simple sentence reminds me that I never talked about her failure to lock up on Saturday, but this is not the time. "No. I'll get it when Karia heads out. Have a good night."

"You too. Nice meeting you Karia." She waves and disappears.

"I should probably get going too." Karia looks apologetic. "I'm supposed to be at my mom's for dinner but since I was driving by, I wanted to see your store."

"Hey it's no problem." I tell her as we make out way to the front of the store. "I'm glad you did. This day has sucked, and you made it better. So, thank you."

She grabs the bag on the counter holding the crystal blue flared vase. "I love this. Blue is my favorite color. I'll see you around."

She walks out the door and I sink into the chair behind the counter. I need to lock up but in a minute. My body is not only wore out from the anticipation I had all day, but also confused from all the caffeine I have ingested in the last hour. I hear the door ding and stand up.

"Did you forget something?" I am expecting Karia but instead I see Chris. The wave of lust is so strong that I have to swallow and grab the counter for balance.

He looks amazing in worn, faded jeans and a black t-shirt. I bite back a laugh when I see that it is a Shenanigans Bail Bonds t-shirt. How ironic is that?

"Hi Whitney," he smiles, and I feel as though my heart is melting. I have no clue what is going on with me. "I forgot you guys closed at five. Thank you for not locking the door so I can pick this beautiful thing up."

When his eyes meet mine over the counter, I swear I feel a zing. Not just any zing but *the* zing. Like in that stupid movie that kids watch over and over with Adam Sandler. The zing is real and holy hell is it awesome. The door dings again and we both turn. I am both equally frustrated and relieved to see Gauge.

"I brought help." Chris smiles and walks over to the vanity. "Come on Gauge, let's load this up so the pretty girl can go home."

Did he just call me pretty? My heart swells as Gauge snorts. "Dude, are you blind? It's just Whitney."

I flip him off and follow them over to the vanity. I deliberately left antique perfume bottles and a gorgeous antique brush on the vanity top. Mainly so I could delay him from loading it up and leaving.

"Excuse me." I deliberately brush against him as I remove the decorative items. God, he smells amazing.

"Not a problem." Chris steps back and turns to Gauge. "Thanks for meeting me here man."

"Anything for your hot mom, Chris." Gauge smiles and I brace myself for the insults to start.

"As long as you don't get caught by my dad yo," Chris stands on one side of the vanity, ready to pick it up. "He will beat you so bad your grandkids will limp."

I move behind the desk and set the antiques down. From this vantage point I can admire discreetly. I'm so lost looking at Chris's ass, he actually lifts with his knees, that it never occurs to me to open the door for them. It's only when they are at the door and Gauge calls out my name that I realize how dumb I must look.

I quickly walk over, brush against him again and pull the door open. I follow them down the sidewalk where they stop at a truck. Determined to be helpful this time, I lower the tailgate on the black Chevy. Chris smiles with gratitude and I feel my legs go jiggly. I step aside as they maneuver it into the truck and lean against it for balance.

"Hey Whit, you can go back inside." God, Gauge is such a dick sometimes. "I mean we got it and all."

I glance at Chris and seeing his attention focused on a yellow strap, flip Gauge off. Deciding I have spent as much time as I can, I turn to Chris. "Thank you for your business Chris. I hope this makes your mother smile whenever she uses it."

He leaves the strap and comes over to shake my hand. "Pleasure doing business with you Whitney." He leans closer so only I can hear him. "Maybe some time we can leave out the business and go strictly to the pleasure."

****

I heard him right, right? I mean I have been replaying this over and over. After I turned red and stammered through goodbyes, I practically floated back into the shop. From there I must have been on auto pilot because I not only managed to make it home without killing myself or anyone, but I also invited over Jo to have wine and cake. I don't even have wine or cake. I stare at my phone in disgust. I mean obviously I have to talk to her. I mean I not only want to bang Chris, but I swear I felt a zing. Before I can talk myself into texting her and canceling there's a knock on the door.

I sigh. It's ok. We will just go somewhere to eat. I wince thinking of Jo's reaction. I mean wine and cake nights are sacred. They are the SOS of our friendships and she knows that when I ask for one that something big is going down. And now I have to look her in the face and say, "oh hey welcome to cake and wine night sorry I don't have either of those two items!" I pull the door open and not only **see** Jo but Karia as well. Karia is holding the cake and Jo has two bottles of wine. I immediately and instantly burst into tears.

CHAPTER SIX: ROAD HEAD

"But the thing is that I don't even know like where to go from here." I take a bite of chocolate cake and wash it down with Moscato. I am so lucky to have Jo. I mean I don't even care – a lot- that she brought Karia without telling me.

Karia the I is silent, points at me with her fork. "Well it seems like you are really into this guy and clearly, the feeling is mutual."

Jo nods in agreement, "look I don't know why you are suddenly all gooey and shit, but this is not you. The Whitney I know, and love would have taken the chance from the moment she wanted him." She raises her glass towards me, "explain."

She has a point. But then again, she doesn't have all the facts. I take a deep breath and let it out, then to buy myself more time I do it again. "Ok." I shove my fingers through my hair wincing when one gets caught on my ring. "Fuck. Anyway. The thing is, it's different with him. I feel something."

Jo is staring at me in a mix of horror and confusion while Karia laughs. "So, you like love him?" Jo is still staring like I suddenly have eight tits and we both ignore Karia the I is silent's question. I decide to just let it all out.

"I have experienced lust before. We all have. That moment when your eyes connect and your heart thunders in your chest and you can think of nothing but that person." I swear I can feel my eyes tear up as I look at her. "I felt that so many times. But this time, I felt something more. A click, a zing. A god damn magnetic pull towards this man." I swallow the lump forming in my throat. "I want more Jo."

Karia, bless her, excuses herself from the table and leaves us alone. Jo pulls me into a hug and whispers "it's about damn time."

****

"Maybe if I sit on it, I can zip it up." I groan to myself as I struggle to pack my overnight bag. Although I rarely ever go out of town to gather inventory for the shop, there is an estate sale I want to check out. I had hoped to talk Jo into a girls trip but somehow it turned into Gauge coming as well. For the first time since I opened up, I am leaving my shop, my baby, in someone else's hands for a few days. Bless Beth. I am also running late. I still have to get gas and pick them up. Exhausting all other options, I sit on the damn case and zip it closed.

I lock up, throw it in the car and practically peel out of the driveway. We will get gas on the way out of town. They may want snacks anyway. I sigh as I turn up the radio. I am going to have a good time. I am not going to feel like a third wheel. This is my trip. I am repeating things to myself over and over desperate to believe them. I have several items I am interested in and that is my focus. Not if Gauge and Jo are making out in the backseat. There will be no road head. I will kill them. I whip up next to the curb and bounce out of the car. I am completely thrown back when my knock is answered by Chris.

I feel my face flame and regret not spending time getting ready this morning. I have nothing on my face, but my eyebrows and they may be sweating off my face right now. Shit.

"Hey!" He beams at me, his beautiful smile turning my insides to mush. He steps back. "Come on in."

I step inside wondering what the fuck is going on and call for Jo. She comes around the corner followed by Gauge carrying matching duffels. Chris takes her bag then follows Gauge out to my car to put the bags in.

"What the hell is going on?" I grab Jo by her arm, not much differently than my mother used to do to me when I was in deep shit.

"We told Chris that we were going with you on a shopping trip for your store and he offered to bring his truck and go with. Plus, you can get to know him better and there's plenty of room at the house we rented."

My legs completely give out. I fall, I fucking fall flat on my back and gape at the ceiling. Surely, she's joking. I can't spend days with this man, in the same car, in the same house. I mean please for the love of God tell me this is a joke.

"Whitney, stop being so dramatic. They are coming up the driveway." She hisses at me and helps me up.

"Dude, you had no right to do this without asking me." I sigh. What's done is done. I force a smile on my face as the door opens back up. "We taking your truck Chris?"

He nods. "If you'd like. Gauge says you planned on renting a U-Haul if you found something and I thought this may save you some money. Plus, I thought getting to hang out with you sounded fun."

Can he get any more perfect? I feel my heart swell up, explode into confetti and land on the floor spelling out C H R I S. I love this man and I hardly know him. This must be what Disney princesses feel, why else would they get married so soon? "That's very sweet of you Chris. Thank you."

We head out the door and I can't believe I missed seeing his truck. "Let me grab my bag."

"We got it already." Gauge gestures with his hands. "I am just that good baby." I roll my eyes at him and walk to the truck. "Oh no." Gauge shoves me to the passenger seat. "I'm sitting in the back with my baby. You sit up front."

My face turns red again and I look at Jo for help. She shrugs and climbs in the backseat. Chris gets in the truck and addresses all of us. "Ok guys a few rules for the road. Under no circumstances does the Backstreet Boys get played. We do not eat Mexican food on the road. When I pee you pee? No special stops. When I sing you sing? If you don't know the words you walk. And last but not least. There is to be no road head unless it is given to me or the navigator."

We all laugh as we pull away from the house. He winks at me. "You like road head Whitney? Or should we stick with snacks?"

I wiggle my eyebrows suggestively. "Well, since you asked." I run my finger along his forearm resting on the center console. "I will stick with snacks. Jerky is the only meat I want in my mouth right now."

He laughs and pulls into the gas station. "A woman after my own heart."

CHAPTER SEVEN: LEFT OR RIGHT

After five hours in the car with this man, I feel like I know him much better. He likes Shinedown and Volbeat but can also handle country. His foot is a little heavy but so is mine. He wears Oakley sunglasses, a nice watch and doesn't text and drive. He sings without worrying what anyone thinks of him and doesn't eat with his mouth open. As we cruise down the street slowly looking for the Airbnb address, I want desperately to hold his hand. Just to see what happens.

"Got it!" He taps the breaks and I feel Gauge slam into my seat.

"Chris!" Gauge bellows. "What's your deal man?"

Jo yawns and stretches. "It looks like we are here."

"Wondrous." Chris whispers as he pulls into the driveway. This man also watches Letterkenny. Am I sure that he is the one for me? That's a Texas size ten four.

We clamor out of the truck, groaning as our muscles stretch. Aside from a few bathroom breaks, lunch and a break so that Gauge and Chris could act like they were humping next to a cactus; we have been confined to the truck. The walk to the front door of the little cottage is welcome. I'm punching in the code on the lockbox when it occurs to me, that there is only two bedrooms. Granted the room I am planning to sleep in has two beds, but oh shit. I open the front door and walk into the pretty all white living room. A kitchen in gray tones with black appliances is to the left. I can see a ladder leading to a loft where Jo and Gauge will sleep, and I can see the door leading to the bathroom.

I point it out to Jo and head that way, closing the door quietly behind me. I sit on the edge of a gleaming claw foot tub and drop my face into my hands. I am going to be sharing a room with this man. He will be mere feet away from me. What if I snore? No. There's no if. I snore like a pig scarfing down slop. I also drool. Oh my God! This is Jo's fault. I'm gonna kill her. No. I'm gonna throw up. As I stand fully prepared to throw up gummi savers and cherry coke, someone knocks on the door.

"Whit, you ok?" I yank the door open and pull Jo into the bathroom.

"No, I am not ok!" Her eyes widen before narrowing into slits. I know that look but I don't heed the warning. "You got me in this fucked up situation. Now I have to share a room with him."

She holds up a hand like a fucking crossing guard. "Shut. Up." She enunciates every word slowly. "I am doing you a favor here ok. He basically told you he wanted to have "pleasure" with you." She does the quotes in the air with her fingers. "You want him, he wants you. You should be thanking me not acting like a freak."

She pulls me into a hug. "Now get out of here or watch me pee cause it's going down."

I laugh and walk out into the hall. Chris and Gauge have hauled in the bags and are sitting on the couch both staring at their phones.

"What do you guys think?" I ask awkwardly.

"I think it's a nice place." Chris answers me absently completely engrossed in his phone.

Hmph. I grab my bag from the pile of others on the floor and walk to my room. I sigh in the doorway. This room is also white bathed in yellow sunlight from the arched window. The two beds are side by side similar to a hotel room with a nightstand in between. Before I can step into the room, I feel Chris behind me.

"They should have done bunk beds." He smiles at me.

I can't help it. I smile back and finish what I hope he was thinking. "So much room for activities."

I step into the room as he chuckles. He follows me, walks to one bed and then the other. I hold my breath when he turns back to face me. "Normally I ask a woman top or bottom, but this time I guess I need to ask you left or right."

I throw my bag on the bed on the right. "So, Chris, are you really that big of a manwhore or do you just talk like one to impress little old me."

He sets his bag down on the other bed and then sits down on it. "Do you want the real answer to that or are you being patronizing?"

I sit down on my bed and face him. "I want to know the truth." I want to know everything about you.

He studies my face, looking deep into my eyes until I feel like he is staring into my soul. Then he smiles again, though it doesn't quite reach his eyes. "I talk like that to hide my insecurities. I have had my heart broken and if I act like women are objects with no feelings it's easier for me to get through the day."

I gape at him. This is not the answer I was expecting. Then he starts laughing and I stand up and hit him in the face with a pillow. "Stop!" he says laughing. "I'm sorry."

I throw the pillow at him and start to leave the room. His hand on my wrist stops me. "I really did have my heart broken. I talk that way because I like to have fun. Women are not objects and there is no two the same." He tips my chin up so I'm looking at him and everything in my body screams "kiss me." Instead he rubs his thumb gently across my lips. "The things is Whitney, I decided that relationships and love were horseshit. Something we feel obligated to have but don't need." I want desperately, so desperately to move my lips just a little to taste his skin. "That is until I walked into your shop and saw you shaking your ass to whatever was playing in your headphones."

He leans down and gently brushes his lips against mine. He lingering, no tongue, just a sweet gentle kiss. Before I can react, he's walking out of the room. "Come on hot stuff, let's see what they want for dinner.

****

They wanted Chinese. After the kiss Jo and I went into the bathroom and did our hair and makeup before dinner. I filled her in on all the details. She didn't have any more answers than I did and by the time we walked out of the bathroom, I had convinced myself it didn't matter. I wouldn't bring it up if he didn't. On the drive over to the restaurant I had sat in the back with Jo and he continually locked eyes with me in the rear-view mirror. I couldn't help but be strangely turned on by it and challenged myself to not look away. Was I going to have sex with this man tonight? Was I going to marry him at some point and have beautiful Thor like babies? He looked away first.

Throughout dinner we flirted. Through eye contact, unnecessary touches and sexual innuendos. It took everything in me to remember that Jo and Gauge were there as well.

"So, what are you guys doing tomorrow?" I asked as I sipped my hot tea.

Jo looked at Gauge. "I don't know. I figured I would go with you to the sale since Chris is here and the boys can go do something interesting."

Gauge looked at Chris. "Do you know what time the strip club opens?" Jo slugged him in the arm.

Chris laughed and took a drink of his beer. "Actually man, I was thinking I would tag a long with Whitney." All of us looked at him in surprise. "If that's cool with everyone."

Jo kicked me under the table. "I need to go to the bathroom. Whitney does too." She practically dragged me out of the booth. As soon as we cleared the door, she shoved me onto a bench designated for breast feeding mothers. "What kind of spell did you put on that man?"

I shrug. I am stunned into silence trying to wrap my head around everything that has happened. In the past five fricking days. That's it. Five days. Unable to stand it, Jo gets up and starts pacing around the bathroom. Her heels click on the marble tile as she goes back and forth in front of me.

"Ok." She stops and faces me. "Maybe this is the real deal."

I nod. I still can't speak. The real deal? How do I know? What do I do? I am not ready for this. And I still have to share a room with him.

"Whitney." She squats down in front of me. "You can do this. We are going to finish dinner, go back to the house and sleep. Tomorrow morning you will shop your ass off, and I will go with you if you want. "

I pull her to her feet and stand up on my own shaky legs. An old woman walks past us and looks at us with disgust. No doubt she thinks we are lesbians in here for a quickie. Old hag. Anyway, I turn back to Jo. "No. You go do something with Gauge. Go exploring. I can handle this."

CHAPTER EIGHT: HEADS OR TAILS

I'm laying in my bed with my tattered tank and boxer set pajamas, counting sheep and pretending that everything I have ever wanted in a man is not on the other side of the room. I can tell he is as restless as I am, the only difference is I lay still as he tosses and turns in an attempt to get comfortable. That man is wearing nothing but black mesh basketball shorts. His chest and abs make me think of Zac Efron and also terribly self-conscious. My body is not worthy of laying underneath his. Not gonna keep me from wanting it and thinking about it but still. I am pretty sure when he took his shirt off that I said "yum" out loud. I tried to hide it behind a quick fake sneeze, but he knows. I know he knows.

"You know I can see your awake right?" His voice is a whisper in the dark.

"How?" Damn, what if that was a test to see if I was awake.

"The moonlight."

"Oh." I had forgotten about the moonlight. It's shining gently making the room take a on grayish glow.

"Want to play a game?"

"A game?" My heart is thundering under my tank top. I'll play any game this man wants.

The lamp on the nightstand flicks on and I blink at the sudden brightness. He is sitting up on the edge of the bed looking at me, fiddling with something in his hand.

"Well not a game exactly. More like a pregame ritual."

I sit up. My nipples stiffen as the tank top moves against my unrestrained breasts. He looks at them briefly before coming back up to my face. "Maybe." I hug a pillow to my chest.

"I have a coin in my hand." He holds a shiny quarter between his thumb and index finger. "I'm assume you watch football."

Who does he think he is talking to? Does he not realize I am an avid lover of football? That I cried when Jamaal Charles retired? That I won $100.00 when the Chiefs won the Super Bowl? Seriously. Instead of going off like I want I feign nonchalance. "Once or twice."

"Ok." He takes a deep breath. "I'm going to flip this coin. If it lands on heads, you do me. If it lands on tails, I do you."

This arrogant son of a bitch! Did he think I was going to have sex with him just like that? I mean I totally am but still! How dare he? Getting myself in check, I smirk at him. "Well it seems to me that you win either way their stud."

"We both win." The intensity of his gaze causes my skin to break out in goosebumps.

I set the pillow aside and stand up. I walk slowly over to his bed and sit down. "I'll flip the coin." I take it from his hand and placing it like the best NFL official send it into the air. I laugh when it lands tails up on the ground. "Looks like you're on top Chris."

When he doesn't move. I reach for the hem of my tank top and go to pull it over my head. His hand holds the tank in place, and I look at him in bafflement.

"This is a marathon, not a sprint." He pulls me towards him. I rest my hands on his shoulders and look down into his face. "Let's take this slow babe. We got all the time in the world."

I stare into his face desperately wondering if this is some line, he uses all the time or if he legit is this amazing. He meets my eyes and arches a brow. I want to badly to win this staring contest but the unwavering gaze of his becomes too much and I have to look away. I lean into him, causing us both to fall into the bed. I bury my neck in his face, loving the way he smells and placing gentle kisses as he holds me.

He gently grabs my hair and pulls me back until I'm forced to face him. "No," he says as I try to go back to his neck. "Here." He leans up and kisses me.

My heart begins racing as our tongues slide over each other. It's pounding with such intensity; I know he has to feel it on his chest. I yelp as he moves quickly still holding me and tossing me onto the bed I just left. He stands in his shorts looking the Greek god of orgasms and for the first time I am incredibly grateful that the light is still on. I wouldn't trade this view for anything. Sitting up, I yank off my shirt before he can stop me. He keeps watching me, saying nothing as I lay back and shimmy out of my shorts. Him watching me is kinda hot and I am beyond ready when he finally takes his shorts off and joins me on the bed.

"Whoa." I raise a leg up to his chest before he can lay down. "No glove no love."

He laughs and stands back up to get a condom. His ass is phenomenal. You know Jax from Sons of Anarchy? Picture that ass but with a tan. I can hardly stand it as I wait for him to get protection. I want him thrusting on top of me as I pull him on close, my hands on that magnificent ass. Wait, why does he have condoms? Was he expecting this to happen? I swear I can feel myself drying up as I contemplate.

He returns from his bag with a little foil packet. He smiles at me and holds it up so I can see it. When I don't smile back, he sits on the bed. "What happened in that pretty little head of yours while I was gone for thirty seconds?" He kisses my forehead and then pulls back to look at me.

I debate not answering and just pouncing on him but that's not fair to him. Plus, I won the coin toss and therefore should not have to do any of the work. I smile sheepishly at him. "I guess I started wondering why you had a condom. Were you planning on this happening?"

He kisses my forehead, the tip of my nose and then my lips before whispering in my ear. "Just hoping."

I don't know if he realized he was quoting John Travolta from Phenomenon or not, but I decide the ride the wave of lust and want instead of analyzing any further.

"I want you." I lick my lips as I watch his eyes change. "Hard and fast. Now."

I lower my leg and allow him to cover my body with his. As we kiss, I feel him enter me slowly. The overwhelming feeling of pure acceptance is something that can't be ignored. I don't want time to think about how well he fits in there. I don't want to think about how my walls are already quivering. I sure as shit don't want to think about my friend and her fiancé somewhere on the other side of the wall. I just want him.

As though sensing, he begins to move and do I mean move! I envision every thrust shoving me further down into the bed. I know I'm getting close and I grab is hips and help gyrate him into me. Yes, my mind screams yes! I clamp down on his shoulder, hard, and I don't know if the sound he makes is from shocks, pain or his own orgasm but it tips me completely over the edge. I lay back into the pillows and look at him. His eyes lock on mine and then we both laugh when we hear Gauge yell from the other room. "Finish her!"

We both laugh but as we untangle and I excuse myself to clean up, I can't help but hope this is only the beginning.

<u>**CHAPTER NINE: ROUND TWO – FIGHT**</u>

"Holy shit dude." Jo is staring at me over her orange juice. "You actually did it. Like full on had sex with Chris."

I take a drink of my coffee and nod. "Indeed, I did."

She looks around to see if him or Gauge are around. "Only once?"

I feel my face flame and I hesitate for only a second before I tell the truth. "Yes." I make a face that can't be described; much like my feelings after. "When I returned from the bathroom, he had his shorts on and was laying on his own bed. So, I just told him good night and climbed into mine."

I didn't tell her that I quietly cried myself to sleep. Being bailed out of jail by her is one thing but telling her about that lonely hour is more humiliation than I can bear. "So yeah, when I got up this morning, he acted like nothing had happened." I scan the room knowing the guys would be back from their buffet trip anytime.

She studies me, and I can see her trying to think out carefully what she wants to say before blurting it out. "So, I would like to say that I am just as confused as you are but that's not true. But I am confused! It seemed – seems like he is really into you. So here is what I am thinking, I am fully ready to tell them both I am going to go with you to the auction."

Before she is even finished, I am shaking my head. Not only are the guys returning with overloaded plates, but I am not going to be a coward and hide from a situation that I created. That is definitely not something that I would do. I greet the guys with an easiness I don't really feel and a smile to match.

"Did you guys leave any for the rest of us?" I find teasing and flirting to be so much easier than normal conversation.

"You snooze you get none or something like that." Gauge answers me as he covers a mountain of French toast with syrup. "What's the plan then?"

Chris answers first as he eats a piece of bacon. I stare at the fingers holding it and a slight shiver goes through my body as I remember them on my body. "Well, I am assuming that Whitney and I are going to need the truck. So, I can drop you guys off somewhere on the way to the auction or you can call an Uber or something."

I sense Jo's movement half a second before I see the pain on Gauge's face and realize that she kicked him not so gently in the shin. I reach over and pinch her thigh as Chris looks on in confusion. Gauge scowls at Jo and then at me, I mean I didn't do anything so what the hell.

"Actually Chris, I was hoping you'd change your mind and go with me to hit a few balls or something. The course here is supposed to be pretty sweet."

Chris looks at me and I feel that damn "zing" again. Suddenly it feels as if everyone is gone and there is only me and him. In our own universe staring into each other's eyes over delicious breakfast foods.

"I planned on going with Whitney today. I told you that." His eyes never leave mine and it's as though he is trying to read my mind. "Unless she would prefer that I didn't."

And just like that, the table and the restaurant are full of people again and three sets of people stare at me waiting for an answer. It's during this time, that I have to ask myself what is it that I really want. Do I want to be a bad ass business owner that does what needs to get done? Do I want to show him that I too can act like nothing happened last night? Or do I want to be the girl that hides behind her best friend and drags her ass to the auction and then makes arrangements to ship everything I buy? Damn, know I sound like I am only using him for his truck.

"Earth to Whitney." Jo snaps her fingers in front of my face. "You zoned out their kid."

I laugh and look at her. "Sorry. I was thinking of all the crap I wanted to buy." I take a drink of my coffee again. "You and Jo go do something fun Gauge. I can use Chris' muscles and his truck."

****

"So, are we just not going to talk about it?" Chris glances at me as we leave the restaurant. I'm staring straight ahead with my sunglasses on and hoping he didn't notice the slight quiver of my chin.

"Talk about what?" Good response if I must say so myself. I can act the same way he did.

I see his hands tighten on the steering wheel. "You know exactly what I want to talk about."

Instead of answering him, I pull out my phone and punch in the address of the auction. "You're going to want to take a right up here."

He puts on the blinker and then mutters something under his breath. I try to keep from saying it but it's just not in my nature.

"What was that?" I push my sunglasses up on my head and glare at him. Maybe a fight will just clear the air and we can move on.

He glances over as he changes lanes. "I said I should have went with Gauge."

"It's not too late pal. Drop me off at the auction and go." The hurt is there but I cover it with anger. "I didn't plan on you being here anyway."

His hands tighten on the steering wheel and I can see a muscle flexing in his cheek. It makes me think that maybe he is literally biting his tongue. I put my sunglasses back on and go back to staring out the windshield. I ignore him until he pulls into a park.

"What are we doing here?" I am fuming and trying to find a way to hurt him without violating my probation.

"You are going to talk to me before I drive you one inch further towards the auction." He smirks, the bastard actually smirks.

In answer I pull my phone out and then open up the Uber app. Who the fuck does this guy think he is? I will walk the four miles before I open my mouth. That plan went quickly out the window when he grabs the phone out of my hand. A red haze forms in my vision as he undoes his seat belt and then lower that magnificent ass onto my phone. My seat belt catches me as I try to attack him, and I slam back into the seat in a huff.

"Whitney." His voice is gentle, and he has removed his sunglasses and set them on the dash.

I ignore him as I undo the seat belt and reach for my purse on the floorboard. He can keep the fucking phone for all I care. The door is open when his voice stops me.

"Please." It's a simple plea and one, damn it, pulls at my heart and has me settling back into my seat. I didn't really want to walk that far in a dress and sandals anyway.

"What?" I can listen without looking at him.

"I know that you're upset with me and I would like to talk about it. Then I promise I will drive you to the auction." He smiles. "I also found a couple estate sales that I think may be of interest to you."

I turn to him in surprise. I love estate sales. But there is no point in being too accommodating. "Ok. Talk."

He picks up his hips and hands me my phone. I take it and put it in the pocket of maxi dress. I watch him and it's obvious that he is struggling with what he wants to say. I watch his adam's apple move up and down as he swallows before speaking.

"I am sorry about however I made you feel last night. It was nothing to do with you."

I look down at my hands and decide that I am due for a manicure. I also think in the back of my mind that if I just stay silent, he will continue. I am fully prepared to wait him out.

"Please look at me."

I turn unable to ignore the request. "I'm looking at you." Why is it that we are never more vulnerable than when a man is opening up to us?

"I just wasn't ready to sleep in the same bed as you yet."

Out of all of the things that I expected him to say, this was not even in the realm of possibility.

"Look, I was in a relationship that I expected to be the last one I was ever in." He looks straight ahead instead of at me. "She was supposed to be it for me."

I can appreciate the honesty but now I am also questioning whether or not I am just the rebound.

"When we were together, it was amazing. More than amazing." He looks back at me and that same zing goes off in my system. "It's like we were meant to be. They way we fit together. But when the time came, I just wasn't able to open myself up that much. I like you a lot. More than a person should like someone they just met and the last thing I want to do is push this too fast."

My heart is thudding as his words touch me. But my defenses don't come down that easily. "So, let me clarify. You have no problem having sex with me, kissing me, seeing me at my most honest self but you don't want to share a bed for about 8 hours."

"You know as well as I do that sex is easy. Our bodies do what need to be done. It's when you add emotions and shit that sex becomes more. And what you and I have is already more. No matter how good the sex is, what I want and need from you is so much more."

My heart has never felt fuller. I slowly slip off the panties under my dress and pounce on him, hitting my ass on the steering wheel and laughing at his surprise.

"What are you doing?"

I smile as I lower his seat and quickly look around the deserted parking lot. "Round two fight."

****

"So, what did you guys do today?"

We have all just met up at Dave and Busters for dinner and to screw around.

Jo is excited that she doesn't give Gauge a chance to talk at all. "We went and did the escape room. And Gauge wouldn't listen to me when I told him that the key to get out was hidden in the skull's eye, so we went around and around."

Gauge rolls his eyes and flags down the waitress, desperate for alcohol.

Jo continues on with her story, all about how her intelligence and wisdom saved them from the escape room. After the waitress takes our order for drinks and appetizers, Gauge is finally able to speak.

"And then because she annoyed the hell out of me so much, we went to some crazy place where you could smash the shit out of stuff. I was able to take a bat to windows and throw cups and plates. Definitely a stress reliever."

We all laugh and then Chris and Gauge began a conversation about how opening one of those in our town would be awesome. I can't help but smile at the two of them. Young boys that get taller but never really grow up. Jo is watching them too and I see her fiddle with her bracelet as she beams in pride at the man she loves. I nudge her.

"Let's go play."

We stand, tell the men to watch the drinks and walk off to the arcade.

"Ok bitch. Tell me everything."

We plant ourselves at two token machines and proceed to collect as many cards as possible. As we pump the bills in, I fill her in on our day. I tell her about the conversation we had in the parking lot, leaving out the hot sex. I tell her about the pieces I bought, the estate sales he researched and surprised me with and how he held my hand the majority of the day.

"I think this could be the real deal." I summarize.

"I'm so happy for you." Jo's eyes are glazed with tears. "But I'm also starving. Let's go eat."

<u>**CHAPTER TEN: ZINGLESS**</u>

"Wow. You got some really great pieces!" Beth is helping me move the new pieces around the store. Chris and Gauge unloaded them into the back for me yesterday when we got back and I'm eager to get them priced.

"Yes, we did!"

I begin working on the price tags while she remove the packing and wipes them down. I am not quite sure where are going to put this stuff, but we have the shop closed today to figure it out. I am thrilled about a singer sewing machine and want to put it near the window with an adorable pin cushion I picked up at an estate sale. Part of the fun is the staging.

"Did you have a good weekend?" I make conversation as I print the tags. I am not only asking on a personal level, but she also worked Saturday, and I am not quite sure what went down while I was gone.

"I did. Saturday day went well. I sold a couple perfume bottles and that little secretary desk. Had a couple looky loos and then I went home, and binge watched Tiger King."

"Who bought the desk?" I am mentally trying to decide what to put in it's place. That didn't clear up a ton of space but certainly enough to showcase the leather stool.

"A rather nice couple. They spent over an hour in here looking around." She shrugged as she cleans a brass mirror. "They said their son had bought them a vanity from here, so they wanted to check it out."

My heart pounds in my chest so fast that all the blood in my body shoots to my brain. I am so thankfully to be sitting. Chris' parents were in my shop. I take a second to be glad I wasn't here. But is that something that is going to happen soon? Are we going to start dating and then meet the parents and all that jazz? I haven't heard from him since he dropped me at Jo's and though he kissed me gently on the lips, I still am unsure of where we are at.

"Hey, are you ok?" Beth has stepped over to the desk and is watching me curiously.

I nod and take a drink of my monster. "Yeah I'm good. Just wondering where we are gonna put all this stuff."

She takes a deep breath and lets it out. "Well there is that. Let's do this thing."

****

By the time seven o clock rolls around, we are both exhausted. The shop is not only rearranged with new pieces mixed with the old but it's also clean. We say our goodbyes as I lock up the deadbolt and then go our separate ways. I'm dreaming of a Jimmy Johns sandwich and a bath before bed. I look like hell and feel even worse. I am sore, I have a headache and I still haven't heard from Chris.

Now that I am not busy, I allow those thoughts to overwhelm me more than I should. And I am not okay with that. I drive through, get my sandwich and blast my music the rest of the way home. I decide to check out that stupid show on Netflix that has taken over my Facebook. I'm going to eat my sandwich, some Doritos and drink wine in the bath.

I stretch before I go run my bath. I only watched two episodes of Tiger King but damn what a mess. I will have to discuss it with Beth tomorrow. I don't know of anyone else that is dumb enough to watch the show. As my bath runs, I scroll through my Facebook, past countless memes about Joe Exotic and see I have a message.

Missing you

It's a simple message from Chris and smiling ear to ear, I reply.

You should.

I am sliding down into the warmth before a thought occurs to me. I have never stalked his Facebook. I mean that is what Jo did to Gauge and also haven't I earned the right? I climb out of the tub and grab my phone. I almost drop the damn thing in my hurry to get back but once I am settled, I begin going through his photos. He seems like a guy who is above the pettiness of deleting old photos. And sure enough, I am right.

His ex is beautiful. Not only is she in multiple photos that she tagged him in, but there just as many that he put up with adorable captions. #loveofmylife #gorgeous #thisisminefellas

I put my phone down on the floor and look at my body. Comparing it to the flawless one that has been with Chris over many years. She's blonde. Big beautiful green eyes. Skin has no acne and I can't spot a single pore. She's tall and skinny, could have been a ballet dancer. And I'm me. I sigh, lean my head back on the edge of the tub and close my eyes. I know Jo makes it seem like I am hot and whatnot but compared to this ex, I don't see it. Her name is Rhiannon like the Fleetwood Mac song. How fitting.

I decide to call it a night. While the bath did wonders for my sore muscles, the hot water drained the last of my energy. That and the sleuthing I did. Which let's be honest is never a good idea. I head to the room without bothering to dry off and barely remember to plug my phone in before collapsing face down onto my pillows. The last thought I have before my eyes close, is that Chris never wrote back.

After a night of tossing and turning along with strange dreams about a demon baby, I start the day full of anticipation. I'm having breakfast with Jo and Karia before heading to the shop. Other than the need to adjust the inventory it should be a pretty chill day. I may message Chris and see if he'd like to do dinner. I'm in my car and about to pull into the parking lot of the diner when my phone shows that Chris is calling me on messenger. And it's in this exact moment that I realize I have slept with a man – twice- without even having his phone number. What has technology done to us?

"Hello?"

"Hello." While my voice was filled with happiness it's obvious that his is not.

"What's wrong?"

There is silence on his end for a full ten seconds and then, "I'd rather talk to you in person. Can you do dinner tonight?"

"Um, sure." We finish making arrangements and I hang up just as I see the other girls go into the diner.

I wait until we are seated and the waitress has left with our orders before I tell them about the call.

"Did I miss something?" Karia asks innocently.

Both Jo and I start laughing and then fill her in on the weekend. It's quite a lot that has happened in a span of days but she handles it well and then gives her honest opinion.

"Maybe, he's ready for it to be a full blown relationship." She nods and thanks the waitress who slides a plate of pancakes covered with berries in front of her. "Maybe he's come to the realization that you guys need to do thing in a more traditional style. Like having each other's phone numbers and getting to know each other before jumping on one another for hot sex."

The waitress coughs and tries to hide the laugh before putting the syrup on the table and leaving.

"Don't be telling the whole world my business." All of us laugh and begin eating with the conversation returning back to the night.

"He wanted to flip a coin and I can't resist a challenge."

"A challenge?" Jo snorts. "From what we could hear through the wall it seems like he didn't a present a challenge at all."

This sends me into spurts of laughter. I find myself unable to stop until I am damn near pissing myself. After a quick trip to the bathroom I come back in a much more somber mood. I don't know if I should ask in front of Karia but I do it anyway.

"So last night I stalked his Facebook and what is the deal with his ex?" I blurt it out before I lose courage.

Jo finishes her bite of biscuits and gravy before she answers. "You shouldn't do that. It leads to trouble."

Karia laughs. "I thought you stalked Gauge."

"Well, that's different." She winks at Karia before addressing me. "Basically he proposed and she said that she wasn't ready for marriage. He thought she needed time but he came home from work and she had moved out. No explanation or anything. That was like six months or so ago."

I can feel the heart that already belongs to him softening until it resembles slime. "Poor Chris."

It's the attitude I maintain through out the day. I feel bad for the guy and I want him to know that I don't plan on hurting him. I want to be honest and upfront. He deserves to know about the zing, about my heart that beats faster when I think about him. As I head to the restaurant I am floating. I have dressed in a belted sundress with cute little pumps. I have on the sexiest lingerie I own and I have shaved everywhere below my eyebrows. He won't know what hit him.

That's why what happened at dinner completely threw me. It plays through my mind again and again as I lay in the beautiful black lacy lingerie and sob into my pillow. The pain has not abated in the several hours since I have been home. It's as though someone froze my heart and then threw it in the air, allowing it to hit the ground and smash into thousands of pieces. Then the jumped on them grinding them into the concrete before letting their dog pee on them.

I force myself to get up and head to shower. I put my phone on repeat blasting "Harden my Heart" on my shower speaker. I give up. The decision is made while I shampoo my hair. From here on out, I am not looking for anybody. I will cut my eyes out before I allow it to feel a zing again. For the rest of my life, I will be zingless. The tears continue falling as I go through my cleansing routine. I have not only lost Chris, but have to face the reality that I never really had him.

CHAPTER ELEVEN: WHAT WOULD WHITNEY DO?

"Look I appreciate the offer but I just don't feel up to it." Six months later, I am still dodging any situation where I may run into Gauge. It's gotten so bad that I no longer go to Jo and Gauge's house at all. And Jo has about had it.

"Dude, you need to let this go. Come to the ugly sweater party please!" Her voice pitches. "Chris isn't even going to be there and quite frankly dude, you weren't even a couple."

Her words slice me so deep, I feel my spine straighten. "Thank you so much for bringing that up Jo. It makes me feel so much better to know that I got heart broken by someone the world sees as irrelevant." I bite my quivering bottom lip and feel the tears come again.

"You know I didn't mean it like that. I just I miss my friend." I hear her voice break and I know that she is trying not to cry. "And I hate that you got hurt but I miss the old Whitney. What would the old Whitney do in this situation?"

"I don't even know the old Whitney anymore. There's only this one." I sigh. "I'll come to the party and I'll be the ugliest one there."

It pacifies her and I hang up, planning the ugly sweater I need to make. The party is this weekend. I walk up front as Beth finishes up a phone call. It's the busiest time of the year for the shop and thanks to events like Small Business Saturday, I am struggling to keep up. Karia even comes in now and again to help out. Things are going well for the store. I guess when I shut down on an emotional level, my professional life just thrives.

"Closing time." Beth sings off key. "You don't have to go home but you can't stay here."

I laugh because its expected. But the truth is that whole thing quit being funny even before Friends with Benefits overplayed it. "Why don't you head out? I'll lock up."

"Thanks Whitney. I'll see you in the morning."

I follow her to the door and pull in the rug. We do not put anything outside during the winter and with the chill, I'm thankful. I'm turning the deadbolt still lost in my thoughts when a sudden knock startles me. It's a huge surprise to see Gauge standing on the other side of the glass. I let him in and then lock the door behind him.

"Hey Gauge." I move behind the register and try to hide the fact that I am completely confused by him being in my shop. Other than that one time with Chris, he's only been in here with Jo once.

"Hey Whitney." He removes his beanie and gloves and sets them on the counter. "I am sorry to come by here when you're trying to leave, but I need your help with something."

Now I'm even more confused but my curiosity is definiftely piqued. "What do you need?" I ask him as I batch out the cards.

He raises his voice to be heard of the paper printing out. "I plan on asking Jo to marry me this weekend. At the ugly sweater party."

My jaw drops so fast, I'm surprised it's still attached to my face. There's also pure joy, knowing how happy this will make Jo. I shut my mouth and come around to hug him. "That's so awesome! I'm happy for you guys!"

He hugs me back smiling hugely. "Thanks!" He lets go of me and looks around the shop. "I need you to help me do it."

"How can I help?" I return to the drawer and pull the credit card receipts to staple to the settlement.

"I want to do it with an ornament or something like that." He clears his throat. "I was hoping you had an antique ornament."

I find my eyes watering. Jo loves Christmas decorations almost as much as Christmas and I can't think of a better way for him to propose. "I do!"

He follows me to a fluffy green tree, I have decorated in the center of a room. He looks through them tree carefully and removes two. One is a little wooden sled and the other is beautiful glass gnome.

"Which one?"

I look at them both and then take the gnome one from his hand. "This one will look perfect with thing ring on the hat. Is that what you were thinking?"

He nods and then putting the sled back on the tree, removes a velvet pouch from his jacket pocket. "It's so hard to hide a box but I have been carrying this pouch around for weeks."

He pulls the drawstring and a beautiful pear shape diamond on a simple gold band pours into my hand. It's very Jo and I can't wait to see it on her hand.

"This is beautiful Gauge."

"Do you think she'll like it?" His eyes are dancing and his joy is contagious.

"She is gonna love it." I take the ring and slide it down the string onto the gnome's crystal hat. "I'll go find the box."

****

It took over three hours to make the ugly sweater dress but I decided it was well worth it as a put it on. I found a dark green dress and wasted no time in decorating it with a bunch of tacky ornaments and tinsel. I have leggings to wear under it covered with brightly wrapped presents. Battery operated Christmas lights cover my boots and match the bulb earrings I am wearing.

Despite me trying not to go, I am filled with anticiatpion. I am going to have a good time. I am determined to enjoy myself and celebrate with my friend. She has no idea anything is coming which makes everything that more impactful. I head out the door, then come rushing back in. I forgot the platter of jello shots. The one thing I was supposed to bring.

The jello shots are the first thing that Jo sees when she pulls the door open minutes later. She has on an ugly sweater asking Todd why the floor is wet. I am early yet the house is already filling up.

"Wow, everyone is early!"

Jo takes the jello shots and puts them a bright red table covered with other food and a santa sleigh full of drinks. I walk around making small talk with people I barely know until I zero in on Karia the I is silent. She is in a blue sweater covered with twinkling lights and blue leggings with snowmen dancing. We take numerous photos in the photo booth and she tells me about Mitch a new guy she has been seeing.

It's nice catching up with her and it saddens me to realize how much I have missed out on by hiding in my house or shop. Gauge comes over and whispers "it's time."

I excuse myself from Karia and then jump into action. I start passing the jello shots around, instructing everyone not to take them yet. When I stop at the couch and notice Chris is sitting there all the color drains from my face. I suck it up, hand him and a shot and keep moving down the line. Once everyone has one, including Gauge and Jo, I stand in the middle of the room and wait.

"Thank you everyone for coming." Gauge addresses the room and has everyone calling out in response. "I would like us all to have a shot together. Not only to celebrate the holiday with friends and family, but also to celebrate the future."

Everyone cheers and takes their shots. While Jo is still trying to get the remainder out of her cup without using her fingers, Gauge removes the gnome from his pocket and gets down on one knee. Everyone quickly realizes what is happening, except for Jo. It's only when the room is completely silent, that she looks up from her shot. Once she spots Gauge on his knee, she drops the shot.

It's ignored as Gauge holds the gnome up, the ribbon hanging from his index finger. Jo looks perplexed and he hurriedly begins to speak.

"I never intended to like you." People laugh including jo who is also quietly crying. "But I did. I liked you so much that I fell in love with you. My heart was no longer mine but yours and my thoughts always came back to you."

She nods, a silent acknowledgement that she too, knows the feeling.

"I knew within weeks of us moving in together that I wanted to never live apart from you. I wanted you to be my wife. So I begin trying to think of the perfect way to propose."

We all watch as he stands and slips the ribbon onto her finger. The diamonds glints in the light and it spins on her index finger slowly.

"This ornament is old. At least seventy five years old." He puts his hand on her face and with his thumb gently wipes away a tear. "That's a long time but not nearly as long as I want to spend with you."

He scans the room, smiling at his parents as well as hers. When he is again facing her, in a choked up voice he asks, "Jo, will you marry me and be my forever?"

We will clap as she says yes and kisses him; holding the gnome to her chest as they hold each other. When they break apart, he slides the ring of the gnome and onto her finger. "I almost forgot."

Everyone comes up and begins congratulating them. After I hugged them both, I decide its time for me to go. Jo will understand and even though this is one of the happiest events, I can't risk running into Chris again.

I remove my purse and jacket quietly from the chair in the kitchen and sneak out the garage door. I'm getting into my car when he speaks.

"Where are you going?"

I don't need the light from the nearby post to know that Chris is talking to me. For the first time in six months. For the first time since he broke my heart in a crowded restaurant.

"You don't have to leave. I will go." He steps closer and I step back in reflex. He puts his hands up palms towards me. "I wanted to be here for my best friend when he proposed. I didn't come to ruin your night. You should stay."

With that he walks away and seconds later I hear his truck start up and drive away. He's right. With him gone there is no reason I need to leave. I return to the party with a heavy heart but a big smile. My best friend has found her forever!

****

It takes me a minute to realize that the knocking is coming from the front door and not in my head. I stumble to the front door and yank it open without looking. Chris' eyes go wide, no doubt because of my appearance and I long to slam the door in his face. Instead I stare at him awkwardly.

"Can I come in?"

"How did you know where I lived?" When he only looks at me, I step aside so he can come in.

I'm in the same ratty pajamas I wore when he and I had spent the night together, I haven't washed off my makeup from the night before and I don't even want to know what my hair looks like. Not exactly how I wanted to have a conversation with this man. But oh well.

"I'm making coffee."

He follows me into the kitchen and sits down at the table. "I followed you last night."

I look at him and then remove a mug from the cabinet about my Keurig. "Ok."

The silence hangs heavy as I make my coffee and open the fridge for creamer. Finally he speaks.

"Damn it Whitney. Do you think it was easy for me to come here?"

The thin tether on my temper snaps and I relish in it. Acting unfeeling and cold has taken it's toll on me and surprise, motherfucker, my probation is over. I'll go back to jail.

"I don't know anything about you Chris. How would I know if something is hard for you or not?"

I pour the creamer into my coffee and stir is much harder than necessary. "Isn't that what you told me that night? That you hardly knew me and that you shouldn't have slept with me when you still had unresolved feelings for your ex?"

I throw the spoon in the sink and then stomp over to my table. I look right into his face and even through all of the anger pulsating in my system, I still feel the zing. It just pisses me off more. "Yeah I am pretty sure that's what you said. And then, you son of a bitch! You told me that she wanted to try again and that you owed it to her and yourself to try to make it work."

Not giving into the urge to flee, I sit at the table and meet his eyes. I do not look away, even after I counted to ten. When I speak it's with a calm soothing voice completely opposite of everything I really want to do. "So, I guess in answer to your question Chris, no. I do not know if this is easy for you."

I stand up and walk back to my coffee. "Would you like some coffee?"

He looks at me and laughs. The expression on my face must have changed because he immediately stops. "You know, I envisioned this conversation hundreds of times and it never looked like this."

He runs his fingers through his hair. "I did tell you that. I felt that I needed to try. I loved her. I loved her so much. But I never felt for her what I felt for you in that brief period of time. It was entirely foreign to me."

I sip my coffee feigning nonchalance as he continues.

"When she came to me and told me that she made a mistake, it was too much for me. The feelings I had for you, you were so intense that I fled to the safety of what I knew. She was familiar, she was safe and she was back. I was trying to do what was right."

"I fail to see why that has brought you to my home unannounced."

He stands up and comes to where I am leaning against the counter in the kitchen. When I make no effort to acknowledge the movement, he leans on the opposite counter.

"Because it wasn't right."

That makes me look at him with suspicion. But I remain stubbornly mute.

"No matter how much I tried, I couldn't stop thinking about you. It sounds stupid but it's like when I looked at you, really looked a felt this magnetic pull."

"A zing." I whisper.

"Yes, a zing." He smiles, "I never miss an Adam Sandler movie, well maybe Jack and Jill. That one sucks."

I turn and set my coffee down, more of a defense move as I no longer can face him. I feel my eyes tearing up with everything he says. I want to badly to believe that this can have a happy ending but history has shown that men are pigs.

Chris approaches the counter and wraps his arms around me. "I want another chance Whitney. I don't care how little I know about you or how little you know about me. I want you. All of you. The good, the bad, the Satan's butthole ugly."

I laugh despite myself and lean back into him.

"But I need to know what you want." He kisses my head and when I don't hit him, whispers in my ear softly. "What will Whitney do?"

I turn and face him, almost headbutting him in the process. "You broke me. For the past six months I have just kinda floated along in life. Feeling nothing, looking forward to nothing."

He nods. "I know."

"The other day Jo asked me, what would the old Whitney do? And the old Whitney would have screwed with your vehicle and shot you with pepper spray."

He laughs softly. "And this Whitney?"

I think on it for half a second before I throw myself into his arms. "The only thing this Whitney wants to do right now is you!"